I0819807

Gray Baker's Newsletter
No.5, Mar. 1976

Gray Baker
Alfred Steber (Editor)

SAUCERIAN PUBLISHER
Original Sources in Ufology

ISBN: 978-1-955087-31-5

9 781955 087315

2022, Saucerian Publisher

PROLOGUE

It is generally a good idea to return to the classics in any genre. This also goes for UFO literature. Rereading a book, or reviewing old documents after ten or twenty years is a rewarding experience. You will discover new data and ideas you didn´t notice before. The reason, of course, is that you are, in many ways, not the same person reading the book the second or third time. Hopefully you have advanced in knowledge, experience, intellectual and spiritual discernment. A good starting point is to reread the UFO classics in order to understand the deeper mystery involved in what happened during that era.

Gray Baker's Newsletter was a leading forum for personal experiences relating to UFOs, psychic abilities, ghosts and hauntings, cryptozoology, alternative medicine, and Fortean phenomena for a devoted readership worldwide. This title is an authentic reproduction of the *Gray Baker's Newsletter* for 1976. Great, but unpretentious, this issue is an extraordinarily rare symbol of what was going on in those early years of the modern UFO phenomena.

Saucerian Publisher was founded with the mission of promoting books in Science Fiction. Our vision is to preserve the legacy of literary history by reprint editions of books which have already been exhausted or are difficult to obtain. Our goal is to help readers, educators and researchers by bringing back original publications that are difficult to find at reasonable price, while preserving the legacy of universal knowledge. This book is an authentic reproduction of the original printed text in shades of gray. **IMPORTANT**, despite the fact that we have attempted to accurately maintain the integrity of the original work, the present reproduction may have minor errors beyond our control like: missing and blurred pages, poor pictures and readers' pencil markings from the original scanned copy. Because this book is culturally important, we have made available as part of our commitment to protect, preserve and promote knowledge in the world.

This book has been formatted from their original version for publication. **IMPORTANT, although we have attempted to maintain the integrity of the issues accurately, the present reproduction could have blurred pages and poor pictures due to the age of the original scanned copy.**

Editor
Saucerian Publisher

Flying Saucer Investigator Gray Barker (May 2, 1925 – December 6, 1984)

Grayson R Barker

in the U.S., Find a Grave Index, 1600s-Current

Want to get involved? Click here.

Report a problem

Detail Source

Name:	Grayson R Barker
Gender:	Male
Birth Date:	2 May 1925
Birth Place:	Braxton County, West Virginia, United States of America
Death Date:	6 Dec 1984
Death Place:	Braxton County, West Virginia, United States of America
Cemetery:	Barker Cemetery
Burial or Cremation Place:	Sutton, Braxton County, West Virginia, United States of America
Has Bio?:	Y
Father:	George Elliott Barker
Mother:	Rosa Lee Barker

159

FORM APPROVED
Budget Bureau No. 33-R012-42

REGISTRATION CARD (Men born on or after July 1, 1924, and on or before December 31, 1924)

(Also for the registration of men as they reach the 18th anniversary of the date of their birth on or after January 1, 1943.)

SERIAL NUMBER W 159

1. NAME (Print) Gray (First) Roscoe (Middle) Barker (Last)

ORDER NUMBER 11,688

2. PLACE OF RESIDENCE (Print) (Number and street) Riffle (Town, township, village, or city) Braxton (County) W. Va. (State)

[THE PLACE OF RESIDENCE GIVEN ON LINE 2 ABOVE WILL DETERMINE LOCAL BOARD JURISDICTION; LINE 2 OF REGISTRATION CERTIFICATE WILL BE IDENTICAL]

3. MAILING ADDRESS Glenville, Gilmer Co., W. Va.

(Mailing address if other than place indicated on line 2. If same, insert word same)

4. TELEPHONE (Exchange) (Number)

5. AGE IN YEARS 18

DATE OF BIRTH May (Mo.) 2 (Day) 1925 (Yr.)

6. PLACE OF BIRTH Riffle (Town or county) W. Va. (State or country)

7. NAME AND ADDRESS OF PERSON WHO WILL ALWAYS KNOW YOUR ADDRESS

Mr. G. E. Barker, Riffle, W. Va. (father)

8. EMPLOYER'S NAME AND ADDRESS

None

9. PLACE OF EMPLOYMENT OR BUSINESS

(Number and street or R. F. D. number) (Town) (County) (State)

I AFFIRM THAT I HAVE VERIFIED ABOVE ANSWERS AND THAT THEY ARE TRUE.

Gray Barker (Registrant's signature)

DSS Form 1 (Rev. 11-16-42) 16—21630-4 (OVER)

Gray Barker (May 2, 1925-December 6, 1984)

Tthe most famous UFOlogist in history , and flying saucer investigator who was the leading figures among flying saucer researchers, who hase challenged the government denial that saucers come from outer space, have been silenced, Gray Roscoe Barker (May 2, 1925-December 6, 1984) was born in Riffle, Braxton County. He grew up in Braxton County and spent most of his life in central West Virginia. After receiving a B.A. from Glenville State College in 1947, he taught school and became a booking agent for theaters in the area.

In 1952, he was working as a theater booker in Clarksburg, West Virginia, when he began collecting stories about the Flatwoods Monster, an alleged extraterrestrial reported by residents of nearby Braxton County. Barker submitted an article about the creature to FATE Magazine and shortly afterward began writing regular pieces about UFOs for Space Review, a magazine published by Albert K. Bender's International Flying Saucer Bureau.

In 1953, Albert K. Bender abruptly dissolved his organization, claiming that he could not continue writing about UFOs because of "orders from a higher source". After pressing Bender for more details, Barker wrote his first book, They Knew Too Much About Flying Saucers, published by University Books in 1956.[4] The book was the first[3] to describe the Men in Black, a group of mysterious figures who, according to UFO conspiracy theorists, intimidate individuals into keeping silent about UFOs. Barker recounted Bender's alleged encounters with the Men in Black, who were said to travel in groups of three, wear black suits, and drive large black automobiles, usually Cadillacs. In 1962, Barker and Bender collaborated on a second book entitled: Flying Saucers and the Three Men. Published under Barker's imprint, Saucerian Books, this book proposed that the Men in Black were extraterrestrials.

Barker published his best-known book, They Knew Too Much About Flying Saucers, in 1956. At various times Barker published flying saucer magazines and newsletters. Through these publications, he contacted people worldwide interested in UFOs, many of whom claimed to have been contacted by aliens.

Over the following decades, Barker continued writing books about UFOs and other paranormal phenomena. In 1970, following the 1967 collapse of the Silver Bridge in Point Pleasant, Barker published his next book, The Silver Bridge. This publication is related to the famous legend of the Mothman sightings. Although he published many other books on strange phenomena, Barker is best known for these two books and a 1983 publication called MIB, The Terror Among Us, about the Men in Black. He was the subject of the 1995 video by Ralph Coon, Whispers From Space. For this production, Coon collected stories from various people who knew and worked with Barker.

Though his books advocated the existence of UFOs and extraterrestrials, Barker was privately skeptical of the paranormal. His sister Blanch explained that Barker only wrote the books for the money, and his friend James W. Moseley said Barker "pretty much took all of UFOlogy as a joke". In a letter to John C. Sherwood, who had submitted materials to Saucerian Books as a teenager, Barker referred to his paranormal writings as his "kookie books."

Barker occasionally engaged in deliberate hoaxes to deceive UFO enthusiasts. In 1957, for example, Barker and Moseley wrote a fake letter (signed "R.E. Straith") to self-claimed "contactee" George Adamski, telling Adamski that the United States Department of State was pleased with Adamski's research into UFOs. The letter was written on State Department stationery, and Barker himself described it as "one of the great mysteries of the UFO field" in his 1967 Book of Adamski.

According to Sherwood's Skeptical Inquirer article "Gray Barker: My Friend, the Myth-Maker", there may have been "a grain of truth" to Barker's writings on the Men in Black, in that the United States Air Force and other government agencies did attempt to discourage public interest in UFOs during the 1950s. However, Barker is thought to have greatly embellished the facts of the situation. In the same Skeptical Inquirer article, Sherwood revealed that, in the late 1960s, he and Barker collaborated on a brief fictional notice alluding to the Men in Black, published as fact first in Raymond A. Palmer's Flying Saucers magazine and some of Barker's publications. In the story, Sherwood (writing as "Dr. Richard H. Pratt") claimed he was ordered to silence by the "black men" after learning that UFOs were time-traveling vehicles. Barker later wrote to Sherwood, "Evidently, the fans swallowed this one with a gulp."

Gray Barker's fame spread after his death in 1984 at age 59. A 1995 video by Ralph Coon recognized Barker as one of the 20th century's leading UFO theorists. Barker's collection is now part of the Clarksburg-Harrison Public Library. When asked once if he believed in flying saucers, Barker replied, "I am not sure, but anything that generates that volume of interest is worth collecting."

No. 5 **Gray Barker's Newsletter** Mar. 1976

Semi-abductee Jennings H. Frederick is the subject of drawing by Gene Duplantier, illustrating the encounter with "Vegetable Man." Page 10.

IN AND OUT OF ZINES

In his book, Planet In Trouble - The UFO Assault On Earth (Exposition Press, 50 Jericho Turnpike, Jericho, NY 11753, 1973) JEROME EDEN discusses UFO writers and observes that although all have their "secret facts," their "pet theories," and "fact-finding" groups, "never a page or a punctuation mark is devoted to the most vital work ever done in the entire UFO field -- that of Wilhelm Reich. Why, Mr. Gray Barker? Why the silence, Mr. John Keel? Why the chronic evasiveness, Mr. Ray Palmer?"

Now I, Gray Barker, can't answer for Keel and Palmer, but I can correct a long-standing ommission at this time, and hope that Eden will overlook my not having tried a hand at the important though complex subject of Wilhelm Reich until this time.

Reich's story should indeed be explored by UFO buffs. It has so many elements of interest: his discovery of a new source of energy, his invention of a device which would "shoot down" UFOs, and his eventual prosecution/persecution by the Government.

I got off on this subject after reading Eden's publication, EDEN BULLETIN (Eden Press, Bx 34, Careywood, Idaho 83809, Qtrly $4.00 dom., $4.50 Fgn, Single copy $1.25) which is devoted to perpetuating interest in Reich's work, to which Eden has devoted much of his adult productive life. The Jan., 76 currentish is 18 pp and should be a must to anybody seriously interested in this subject.

I first heard about Reich in the spring of 1957 when I had just returned home from a publicity tour promoting my book, They Knew Too Much About Flying Saucers (Saucerian Press, Inc., reprinted 1975, $9.95), and received a puzzling phone call. A woman with a husky, commanding voice told me her name was Dr. Eva Reich and pleaded that I might be able to help her father, who had been unjustly imprisoned because of his studies of flying saucers. She desperately wanted to know what Bender had found out and who silenced him.

I had never heard anything about Reich's work at that time and unfortunately I remember little of what his daughter told me. What memory is left indicates that I probably classified the conversation as a crank call and got off the line as quickly as I could. I will always regret not having heard out more completely and not being more sympathetic to the daughter of a man who was either mad, a genius, or both. A few months later, on Nov. 3, 1957, he would die in prison, branded a quack by the Federal Drug Administration, and leaving his assistants and followers fragmented and confused, as the smoke from his burning books spiraled upward to meet and blend with the ever encroaching DOR clouds, with their deadly energies threatening to bring universal drought, and a sickness to mankind that was both physical and psychological.

AT 3:30 P.M. ON JANUARY 6, 1941, A GUANT FIGURE IN A SOMBRE GREATCOAT carrying a weird optical device rang at 115 Mercer St. in Princeton, N.J., and addressed the housekeeper in gutteral English.

Albert Einstein appeared and welcomed Dr. Wilhelm Reich into his study. The genius of mathematics knew his visitor through his reputation. Born in Austria, and having studied with Sigmund Freud, he was internationally known for his books and papers on psychiatry, science, history and sociology. He had fled his homeland during Hitler's rise to power and made his home in the United States, and at that time was teaching Experimental and Clinical Psychology at New York's New School for Social Research.

After a few pleasantries Reich briefly sketched some of his theories to his host and then suggested they draw the blinds and turn out the lights. When their eyes adjusted to the darkness Reich handed Einstein his device which he called an ORGONOSCOPE and the latter was amazed as throughout the darkened room he saw the scintillating rhythms of ORGONE Energy, flickering like a thousand fireflies. Reich explained that

ORGONE was a "mass-free primordial, pre-atomic energy, a cosmic energy filling all space, acting within the living organism as the biological, Life Energy." He told how he had invented a device to accumulate and concentrate the energy and showed Einstein his records which indicated that temperatures near his accumulator were consistently higher than the surrounding atmosphere.

"If your notes are true," a shaken Einstein told Reich, "you have exploded a bomb in physics!"

The two men talked excitedly for five hours in German, their native tongue, and Einstein promised that if the theories proved to have merit he would use his prestige to aid Reich in bringing his findings to the attention of the scientific community.

Two weeks later Reich personally delivered an Orgone Energy Accumulator which he called "ORACCU" (Reich developed a colorful terminology for his discoveries, usually involving abbreviations -- see Glossary). He gave Einstein a preliminary demonstration which tended to confirm his theories, but insisted that the latter carry out his own independent experiments with the ORACCU.

One month later Reich would be infuriated and distraught when Einstein wrote that an assistant had found an "objection" to the experiment and that the increase in temperature could be "explained." With the letter Einstein's interest terminated.

To this day many of Reich's supporters insist that his imprisonment was due to political reasons. Indeed there may have been some complex elements involving the Cold War here, during the mid-fifties, as there were with UFOs in general at that time.

Before Hitler's rise to power Reich could have been classified as a leftist, as were most of his academic colleagues. Later Reich rejected Communism, one of the reasons why he was in turn rejected by many of his former associates. But he also was opposed to Fascism and was outspoken in his views. It is interesting to note that Einstein's assistant, who pooh-poohed the ORACCU and who may have tricked his superior into ignoring it, returned to Communist Poland to teach in 1950. Reich believed that he had delivered many of his discoveries, as yet unrecognized in the U.S., into the hands of the USSR, and claimed that the ORACCU was being used in Soviet medical research. In fact anybody who is "Communist-conspiracy-oriented" (and I'm not saying you're a kook if you are) can find a wealth of rich material for the intellectual mill in the history of Reich).

In 1942 Reich founded The Orgone Institute, the home for his new science of ORGONOMY, on a 280-acre estate in Rangley, Maine, which he characteristically christened "ORGONON."

And it was at ORGONON that the fateful ORANUR experiment was carried out. The experiment led Reich to two important discoveries: that his ORGONE energy could nullify atomic radiation, and <u>that visitors from outer space were secretly dumping a deadly form of energy into Earth's</u> atmosphere!

On January 5, 1951, Reich put some radium into a large scale version of his ORACCU and left it there, for five-hour periods, for a week. Then all hell broke loose. The Geiger counter went wild and jammed. The metal-lined buliding in which the experiment was housed glowed at night. One physician assistant went into shock. Mice used in the experiment died Reich fell ill and hovered between life and death for weeks. The radium was removed and buried. When it was later dug up it had lost an amazing amount of its power, indicating to Reich that ORGONE energy could be employed to combat rising world radiation levels caused by nuclear bomb testing. The spectacular manifestations witnessed during the experiment were due to ORANUR, a highly stimulated or energetic state of ORGONE energy, brought about by the ORGONE's contact with radiation.

During the terrifying ORANUR experiment Reich accidentally pointed a series of ordinary metal pipes, grounded to a deep well, at the threatening black clouds which hung over ORGONON, and they dispersed. He christened the device the CLOUDBUSTER, and employed it from that point on, not only to disperse the dangerous DOR clouds, but in his soon-to-be-declared war on space ships from other planets!

Reich's DOR (Deadly Orgone Energy) Clouds were saturated with MELANOR, a black powdery substance which was cosmic ORGONE energy from outer space. This form of ORGONE is devoid of water and oxygen and is hungry for these substances, and robs them from rock oxides, the bodies of mankind and living vegetation. It dehydrates the soil, as well as humans and plants, and is causing droughts and encroachments of deserts.

UFOs had been appearing over ORGONON since 1951, though Reich took little interest in them until he read Maj. Donald E. Keyhoe's Flying Saucers From Outer Space in 1953 (Henry Holt & Co., NY, 1953).

Reich concluded that the UFOs (which he termed "EAs") utilized a form of ORGONE energy for propulsion. At first he had thought the DOR clouds had some connection with atomic experiments, but upon study of the EAs he concluded that the deadly MELANOR was not related to nuclear radiation but was a waste product dumped into the atmosphere by the CORE MEN (his term for EA occupants). He mounted an offensive against the saucers, and utilizing ORUR, a by-product of his ORANOR experiment, in connection with the CLOUDBUSTER, turned the device against the invaders. Whenever he pointed the CLOUDBUSTER at the glowing objects they would change colors and retreat.

Reich's major effort at weather control took place near Tucson, Arizona, on a 50-acre location which he called LITTLE ORGONON. This experiment sought to test the efficacy of the CLOUDBUSTER in lessening desert encroachment, not necessarily to induce large amounts of rain.

Reich, who would drive to the West Coast in order to observe DOR and drought conditions on the way across country, sent his staff ahead of him to prepare the site. On the way two of his associates, who were driving a truck containing several CLOUDBUSTERS, were attacked by EA's

---

A REICHENESE GLOSARY

ORGONE: Reich's mass-free primordial, pre-atomic energy, a cosmic energy filling all space, acting within the living organism as the biological Life Energy.

ORACCU: The Orgone Energy Accumulator.

ORGONASCOPE: A device for viewing ORGONE in a darkened room.

ORGONOMY: The science of ORGONE energy.

ORGONON: Reich's Maine estate where ORGONE energy studies were carried out.

ORANOR: A highly excited state of ORGONE energy as a result of contact with nuclear materials.

DOR: Deadly ORGONE erergy because of the presence of:

MELANOUR: Cosmic ORGONE energy from outer space devoid of moisture.

EA's: Space Ships (E=Energy, A=Alpha; also Reich thought of this term as an abbreviation for "enigma".)

CORE MEN The occupants of the Space Ships.

ORUR: Orgonomic Anti-Nuclear Radiation (Nuclear energy made harmless by exposure to ORGONE-ORANUR.) This substance adds effectiveness to the:

CLOUDBUSTER: A device for dispersing DOR clouds and for combatting the CORE MEN.

HIGs: Hoodlums in Government.

BOSCO: A device maybe similar to the CLOUDBUSTER used by Karl Hunrath.

LITTLE ORGONON: Desert site near Tucson, Arizona, where CLOUDBUSTER experiments were carried out.

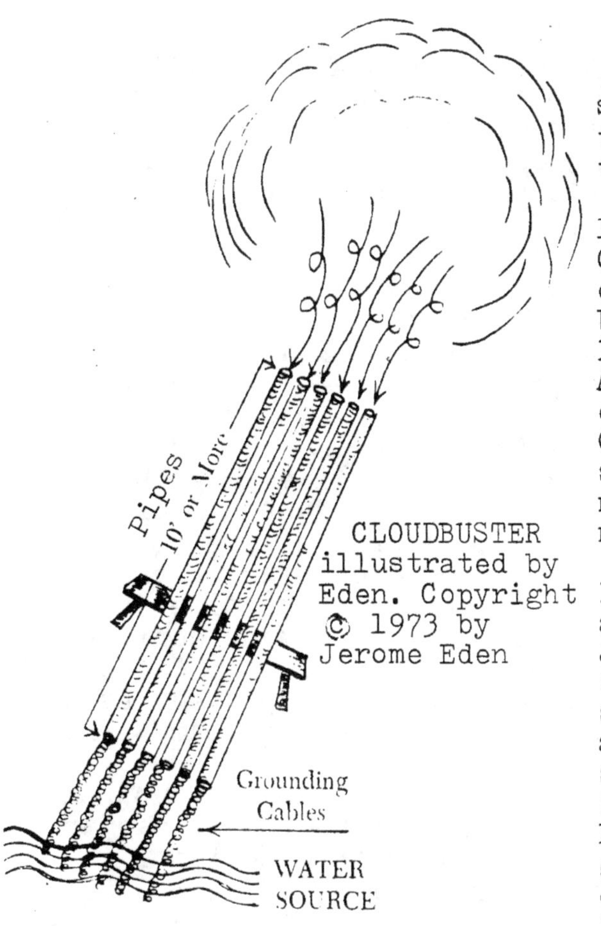

CLOUDBUSTER illustrated by Eden. Copyright © 1973 by Jerome Eden

which they saw hovering below heavy storm clouds. The CORE MEN induced a torrential downpour which almost wrecked the truck.

Reich's journals claimed that the lengthy cloudbusting experiments at LITTLE ORGONON created marked improvements in the desert environment and soon after they began his staff noted the greening of plant life that previously had been dried up. At the desert site Reich continued his war on the EAs, though not without casualty. One of his associates, Robert McCullough, suffered paralysis of the right leg while manning the CLOUDBUSTER against the spacemen.

At the risk of getting sidetracked, I must add the following tid bit which has always fascinated me since I read it in James W. Moseley's The Wright Field Story (Saucerian Books, 1971), which tells of the strange disappearances of Karl Hunrath and Wilbur J. Wilkinson. They were never seen again after announcing they were keeping an appointment to meet a flying saucer. Prior to their disappearance they spent a great deal of time in the company of Jerrold Baker and George Williamson, at the residence of George Adamski on Mt. Palomar in California.

Hunrath drew the ire of Adamski when he exhibited a black box which he, an electrical engineer and an expert in electromagnetism, claimed could be used to duplicate the magnetic power by which the saucers operated and to cause them to crash. Like Reich's ORACCU, Hunrath's black box had a name -- "BOSCO" -- a weird moniker that likely is an abbreviation for some longer term. Whether or not it worked we may never know. Adamski, who believed the UFOs came in peace and friendship, was afraid Hunrath might use the device to harm his interplanetary friends, and this and other differences led to his throwing out the foursome a few days later -- not a bad idea since it would seem that they had been freeloading on his hospitality for an inordinately long time. Williamson, the scholar among his small group, very likely had heard of Reich's work, and it sounds as if there may have been a connection between BOSCO and Reich's CLOUDBUSTER (Greenfield: see detailed Reichenese Glossary previous page).

From the time of the LITTLE ORGONON experiments the remainder of Reich's life was anticlimax and tragedy. The Federal Drug Administration ended a long investigation by seeking a court order to prevent Reich from employing his ORACCU for the treatment of disease, and to destroy his books and writings which described the device and treatments.

There is little doubt that Reich could have avoided prison had he obeyed the resulting court order. It is concievable, though unlikely, that the court order could have been averted had Reich fought the case -- but he refused to appear in court to answer the charges, on scientific, moral and philosophical grounds, reflecting personality difficulties that prevented many from understanding him and alienated him from many would-be supporters.

Although books are protected under freedom of speech in the Constitution, and although one can get by with making most any medical or health claim in print, medical devices are not so protected. An exception, whereby books may be banned or destroyed, does exist, however, when they are published in connection with such a device, constituting "mislabeling" in the language of the FDA. In such cases both the devices and the books may be prohibited and destroyed. A long list of Reich's books were ordered destroyed, many of them having little or no connection with the ORACCU. Naturally it was impossible to destroy all copies, and these books are gradually being reprinted. EDEN BULLETIN carries bibliographic references and news of these reprints.

Reich did not obey the court order and was imprisoned on contempt charges, after losing appeals which reached the Supreme Court.

Many of Reich's supporters believe there was a sinister plot behind his conviction and imprisonment, because of his political ideas, and, of course, the AMA. In his book Eden creates his own Reichnese, while describing the federal prosecutors as "HIGs" (hoodlums in government). Though superficial reading of some of the trial records indicate that he was tried constitutionally and fairly, there are some unusual elements. For example, Peter Mills, the prosecuting attorney for the Government, was originally the attorney for the Wilhelm Reich Foundation, the Orgone Institute, as well as being Reich's personal attorney at the time. Having had access to the inside of Reich's operations, including many confidential details, he had a distinct advantage over any other lawyer in prosecuting the case. I don't know the ethics involved here, or trial procedures at that time, but his selection as prosecutor in the case would seem to have been improper.

Re-reading this fractured coverage of a large and complex subject we realize that our treatment may make the scientist read like a madman, and of course he may have been. Or he may have been a scientist far ahead of his (and our) time. Despite his brilliant mind, Reich was not able to communicate well with his associates and the scientific community at large. He refused to delegate much of his work which might have led to a greater understanding of it. During the legal procedings that led to his jailing and death Reich was given a court-ordered psychiatric examination and declared sane.

Jerome Eden is the most voluble of the many students and supporters of Reich who are still active. The CLOUDBUSTER pictured on the preceding page is from Eden's book and is based on the original design. Although it is relatively simple, and could be constructed by almost anybody who has a little mechanical abilility, Eden urges us "not to play around with a cloudbuster". If not used in a proper manner the device can cause hurricanes, twisters, floods and other weather anomalies. Eden is registered with the U.S. Government as a person engaged in weather control experiments and regularly employs the CLOUDBUSTER in his work. Use by any person not duly registered could also constitute a violation of law.

Finally, Mr. Eden, now that we HAVE finally come up with a discussion of our long-neglected Reich interest, how about correcting any errors I'm sure I have made? I will be glad to publish them.

And, mirroring Eden's words, how about you, Mr. Palmer? How about you, Mr. Keel?

UFO MAGAZINE NEWS BULLETIN (3403 West 119th St., Cleveland, O 44111, Qtrly $2) is published by Rick R. Hilberg, who is assisted by his wife, Carol J. Hilberg and well-known Ufologers Edward M. Biebel, Beth Biebel, Robert S. Easley and Thomas L. Nealings. Offset printed from typescript, averages 4 pp. An article in a recent issue describes a sighting by Christopher Columbus' crew, who grew panicky until the Captain persuaded them it was a good omen signalling the end of their fateful voyage. Hilberg is one of the organizers of the Congress of Scientific Ufologists (later the National UFO Conference), the Annual MYSTICON, and the "super secret" but we're treading on confidential ground as to the latter.

The #2.00 enclosed for dues is being returned with this application. This should in no way effect our personal relationships. I enjoyed our visit at W.I.U. Walt

MUTUAL UFO NETWORK
(MUFON)

40 Christopher Court
Quincy, Illinois 62301

APPLICATION FOR MEMBERSHIP

Name JAMES W. MOSELEY Age 42 Occupation INVESTMENT MANAGER

Address P.O. Box 163 City & State Fort Lee, N.J. Zip Code 07024

Telephone - Home: A/C 201-943-1924 Business: A/C 201-945-3148

Please enter your highest formal educational level 2 years of college

Other fields of specialized training Spanish, typing, editing - 14 YEARS EDITOR OF S.N.

Are you a Radio Amateur Operator? no Call Letters ____

Do you have a Citizen Band radio? no Call Letters ____

List other UFO organizations to which you belong National UFO Conference (Chairman)

What is your prime interest in the study of the UFO phenomena? an objective study of the relationship between UFO's (if any) and other phenomena, such as poltergeists, monsters, ESP, etc.

Have you concentrated your research to a category? no
If so, what is your specialized field of expertise? ____

Are you an amateur astronomer? no Model of Telescope ____

Considering your education, experience, occupation, and available personal time, in which capacity do you feel that you could best serve MUFON in UFO research?

Consultant ✓ State Director ____ State-Section Director ____
Field Investigator ✓ Amateur Radio Communications ____
Astronomy ____ SKYLOOK Reporter ✓ Other supply clippings

Date 2/5/74 Signature James W. Moseley

* *

Appointed to the position of ____
and ____ on ____ (date)

Membership card issued ____ (date) Annual Dues Received ____ (date)

Recommended by ____

Walter H. Andrus, Jr.
Director, MUTUAL UFO NETWORK

Jim: Thank you for your interest in MUFON. The Board of Directors of MUFON did not approve your application. They felt that your past record would be detrimental to the goals and objectives of the organization. Walt Andrus

The preceding page reproduces a MUFON membership application form as completed by James W. Moseley, and that organization's rejection noted by Walter Andrus in the upper left and lower right corners. In the following article Gene Steinberg defends Moseley's "past record" referred to by Andrus. Because of Moseley's reputation in the UFO investigative field and the unpopularity of the MUFON Board of Directors' decision among rank and file MUFON members, the turn down has become a controversial issue in Ufology. Reader comment will be appreciated and responsible comment by interested parties in rebuttal will be given equal space. G.B.

Guest Soap Box

LET'S LOOK AT THE RECORD

By Gene Steinberg

Jim Moseley doesn't conform to the traditional image of a martyr. He doesn't breathe fire and brimstone down on those who have committed real or imagined wrongs against him, nor does he seem particularly perturbed over the fact that, in the UFO field, he hasn't had exactly fair treatment.

If anything, Jim is very cool and collected when he discusses the refusal of the Mutual UFO Network to allow him to join.

"I'm very philosophical about it," he says with a wry grin, puffing away at an ever-present cigarette. "NICAP cancelled my membership ten years ago, yet I still managed to get hold of their publications. MUFON is simply the NICAP of the 70's. Ten years from now some other organization will rise to take its place.

"And they'll probably try to keep me off their membership rolls too," he chuckles.

So it's very clear that Jim Moseley won't be making a cause celebre over the fact that -- unlike just about anyone else in the world -- MUFON will not permit him to be a member.

The logical question is why, and the answers are very clouded indeed.

Let's look at the record, as the politicians say, and see if Jim has done anything in the UFO field that would make a national organization shy away from admitting him as a member.

Jim Moseley, the wealthy son of a former Army Deputy Chief of Staff, first got the UFO bug in the early 1950's. He became so fascinated by the lure of the mysterious discs and the possibilities they posed that he traveled all across the country over a period of several months to find out just what it was all about.

If someone had a well-publicized sighting or claimed to have some knowledge of the origin of UFOs in those days, as likely as not, a tall, wiry young man would be at their door to find out about it.

In the course of his wanderings, Jim accumulated a vast collection of notes of sightings and interviews with the prominent UFO personalities of the time. He wanted to write a book, and a major New York publisher nearly bit at the tantalizing bait. But another, better known writer was there first, and Jim was left with his notes and his travel bills (Many of these notes were later published by Saucerian Books, as The Wright Field Story, in 1971).

Jaded but not really bitter, the resourceful young man took a step he has never regretted -- he started his own UFO magazine. First it was called NEXUS (Latin for "connecting link"), but when readers couldn't identify with the title, Moseley latched on to the more commercial sounding SAUCER NEWS.

From the very beginning, the magazine was an open forum for all kinds of viewpoints on UFOs. One issue might contain an in-depth probe into the claims of a new saucer contactee, cheek by jowl with a very carefully documented reports of strange lights in the sky seen by an airline pilot or other qualified observer.

So if in SAUCER NEWS he committed any sin at all, it was to keep the magazine uncommitted, except for his editorial page. Whether the writer agreed with Jim or not, he found a place in which to express his views.

In fact, Jim is credited with being the founder of the growing "middle Ufology" movement, a loose federation of investigators from around the world who are open minded enough to consider all aspects of the UFO question, free from organizational bureaucracy and restrictions of thought.

This attitude soon got him in trouble with both conservative and liberal UFO fans alike. The conservative -- the nuts and bolts person who thinks UFOs are spaceships, but dismisses all but the most basic eyewitness report of UFO occupants -- felt Jim was detracting from the serious atmosphere of UFO research by allowing contact claims to appear in the pages of SAUCER NEWS. The liberals didn't much like Moseley either, because of the attempts of some S.N. writers to debunk some of the well publicized reports of meetings with intelligent Venusians or Martians.

But as the years passed, it soon became clear to all but the most committed of any particular Ufological persuasion that this middle-of-the-road approach was the best one to take, at least until there was some concrete evidence around as to just what the UFO enigma was all about.

The vast influx of people into the field in the 1960's was largely credited to magazines like SAUCER NEWS -- where someone could be exposed to the whole spectrum of UFO evidence without pressure to take any particular side in the controversy.

But in 1965, Jim published an article that made him the enemy of the arch-conservative NICAP. It was "A Resolution for a Better NICAP." The document was authored by UFO theorist Allen Greenfield of Atlanta, Ga., and this writer, and signed by many prominent people in the field. It was simply a plea for NICAP to open up its collective mind to a wider range of UFO information, and to stop being so authoritarian in the way it treated those who didn't subscribe to all its policies.

NICAP's leadership didn't consider that Jim might not have written the resolution, or even been the motivating force behind it. They cancelled his membership, in the form of a vitriolic letter from then-director, Major Donald Keyhoe.

As for those who signed the resolution (particularly those who wrote it), they didn't hear so much as a whisper from NICAP about the status of their memberships.

Depite NICAP's emotional reaction of the time, they later adopted most (if not all) of the recommendations in the resolution, without once acknowledging the source of their "enlightened" ideas.

Jim joined under an assumed name -- and later, when he tried to rejoin under his own name, he was again turned down.

Comes the 1970's and the establishment of MUFON.

Actually, MUFON started pretty much as a splinter group of the Arizona-based APRO. It seems (according to a reliable source) that MUFON head Walt Andrus wanted to form a Midwest UFO Network within APRO in which to coordinate UFO information in that section of the country. APRO's leadership would have none of this, however, perhaps fearing a rival in its midst. Anyway, Andrus started the organization on his own. Later, as the group became more national in scope, the word "Midwest" was dropped in favor of "Mutual."

As far as anyone knows, Jim Moseley never wrote "A Resolution for a Better MUFON,' nor was he involved in any dispute -- ideological or otherwise -- with any person in any executive position in the organization. In fact, Jim has all but retired from UFO research, although of late he has indicated plans to publish a newsletter and step up his activities in other ways.

Jim recalls that he only received the best of treatment when he met personally with MUFON leaders at a UFO symposium several years ago.

He's never publicly or privately attacked them.

So what's it all about anyway?

Perhaps Jim's run-in with NICAP in the 1960's has been handed down to MUFON in some distorted form. Perhaps the organization's leadership didn't condone some of the ideas expressed in SAUCER NEWS, even though Jim's publicly stated opinion on UFOs differs little from theirs.

The record shows that Jim Moseley has never done anything to threaten the security or well-being of MUFON. While the organization may legally be able to bar anyone from membership, since it is a private corporation, morally they have no grounds at all.

The record speaks for itself.

VEGETABLE MAN -- A SEMI-ABDUCTEE?

Investigated and Reported by Gray Barker

(Cover and Illustration above by Gene Duplantier)

North of Fairmont, W. Va., U.S. Rt. 19 grows crooked and confused. The local traffic not able to take the I-79 bypass picks its way carefully around the treacherous curves, especially in winter. You reach the little hamlet of Rivesville to find nobody in the streets on this snowy afternoon.

You're trying to reach the Grant Town area in the back country, but road signs are sparse and of little help: unless you are a resident of this area it is difficult to find your way. And there is not much reason for an outsider to go there anyway.

But I was on a unique mission to see Jennings H. Frederick, amateur rocket expert lately turned UFO investigator. His efforts to help crack the UFO mystery had come about not by choice, but due to a necessity for proving to himself his own sanity!

For Frederick had been a victim of a syndrome familiar only to the most perceptive UFO investigator: he had not only experienced multiple sightings, but his mother had sighted a strange craft with occupant; he had encountered an abominable green creature and had been visited by the MIB, hopefully in a dream, but with the mark of the needle in his arm for days afterward.

As I picked my way over the unfamiliar side roads, hoping the snow showers would halt, I mused over the landing report we had discussed over the phone.

On April 23, 1965, Ivah Frederick was cleaning up the breakfast dishes after getting the children off to school and her husband to the day shift at the mine. She glanced out the small kitchen window and saw what she first thought was a child in the hillside pasture field above the house. Fearing the child might be injured if it tried to climb over the electric cattle fence, she ran onto the front porch for a better look.

There her concern turned to amazement and shock. A saucer shaped aircraft hovered near the ground and then landed. Running downward from it, through what appeared to be an elevetor and doorway, ran a dark green colored cable. Attached to the end of the cable by a connection at its stomach area was a small black or dark green colored creature. It appeared to be more animal, or even Satanic, than human. It was collecting grass and dirt and stuffing them into the small bag it carried, and it didn't seem to be aware of her observing it. It was unclothed, had pointed ears and a tail. She could see no mouth or other facial characteristics, though it was about 200 yards away and she was very frightened and watched it only a short while before fleeing inside the house, getting into bed and pulling the covers over her eyes, "hoping it would go away."

She was able, however, to supply a few additional details: she estimated the craft was about 10 ft. in diameter and about 5 ft. in height, not counting the stem, or elevator which was about the same height. It was cream and silver colored, with rows of windows underneath a dome or "crystal canopy" on the upper surface which sparkled in the morning sun. The machine rotated in a clockwise direction while emitting a loud humming or buzzing sound.

After about 15 minutes Mrs. Frederick recovered enough composure to venture another look out the kitchen window, just in time to see the creature step into the stem of the craft and disappear. The craft then rotated faster, the buzzing sound got louder, and suddenly it rose, "like a feather," straight up out of her view.

When Jennings, the oldest son, came home from school and heard her story, he hastened to the hillside to investigate. There he found a depression in the ground where the stem of the craft had sat, and estimated that the weight must have been more than a ton. He also found claw-like tracks of the creature which he estimated weighed about 45 lbs. (See drawing at right made by Frederick). He also found some hair samples in the footprints, and sent these, along with plaster-of-Paris impressions and photographs of the area to the Air Force. The AF replied with an inane explanation -- a weather balloon -- and never returned the physical evidence. This evidence indicated that his mother hadn't been dreaming, and the complexity of her account indicated a technology far beyond her limited education and experience.

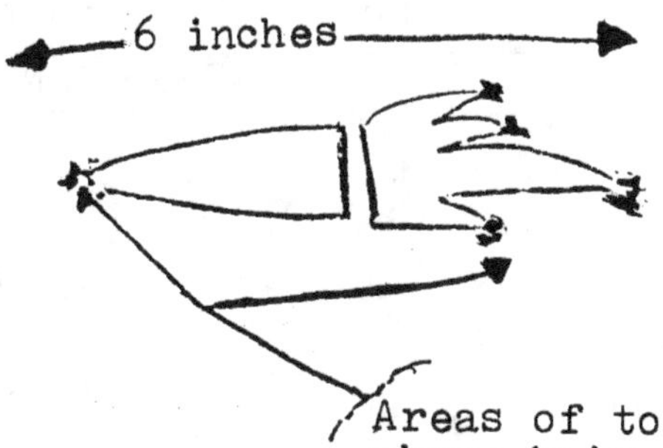

The vast construction of the old mine, its abandoned elevator rising spectrally in the storm like some Dark Tower from a Keel extrapolation, loomed ahead of me, and I knew I was nearing Grant Town. I shuddered as I realized that many miners still lay entombed in the serpentine catacombs below, sealed off when the old mine, years ago, had belched forth flames and poisonous fumes from an explosive hell below. In a field to my right some thin cattle crouched in a tight group, trying to shield themselves against the storm, chewing cuds of dry hay with only cloudy regurgitated rememberances of a summer's greenery in their brute minds dulled by winter.

But it had been in the bright lazy days of late summer when Frederick had encountered something so outrè and outlandish he had frozen in his tracks, his terrestrial weapon hanging limp and useless in his left hand. From the lack of a better description, Frederick called it "Vegetable Man."

I sat in Frederick's comfortable living room, as his wife did sewing in the kitchen, and his two-year-old daughter ambled and cooed around the modest apartment, sometimes pausing to play with our notes and files, and the UFO books I had brought for reference.

Frederick was a young, husky, good-looking man in his early 30's. His language, precice and clear like the notes he had sent me, hardly gave hint of his rural upbringing, never employing the localisms and brogue which often crept into my own speech. He certainly wasn't a kook or candidate for the nut house -- though deep beneath the surface of his calm demeanor I could sense something else, maybe a note of controlled urgency, or maybe pangs of suppressed terror.

The encounter with Vegetable Man occurred in mid-July of 1968, just before he was to enter the Air Force. It was a beautiful day and he had been hunting unsuccessfully for wood chuck. As the sun was setting he decided to return home, and near his father's property line he stopped under some maple trees. He removed the arrow from his 45-lb. bow and transferred both to his left hand to rest his arm.

As he paused he heard a high-pitched jabbering, much like that of a recording running at exaggeraged speed. He believed he could understand the words, but he may have experienced telepathic communication:

"YOU NEED NOT FEAR ME. I WISH TO COMMUNICATE. I COME AS FRIENDS. WE KNOW OF YOU ALL. I COME IN PEACE. I WISH MEDICAL ASSISTANCE. I NEED YOUR HELP!"

Stunned and puzzled, he reached with his right arm for a handerchief in his hip pocket to wipe his perspiration. He winced. At first he thought his hand had become entangled in a wild berry briar and he quickly withdrew his arm.

Attached to his wrist was what looked like a thin, flexible right hand and arm, of a green color like a plant, and the size of a quarter coin in diameter. The hand, which terminated with three fingers about seven inches long, and with needle-like tips and suction cups, grasped his arm more tightly and punctured a blood vessel. He heard a suction sound and knew blood was being drawn.

Frederick turned to see a terrifying being with semi-human facial features, though there the resemblance ended. Its slanting eyes were

---

WE THANK GENE DUPLANTIER FOR ANOTHER MARVELOUS COVER ILLUSTRATING FREDERICK'S EXPERIENCE (IT SCARES YOUR EDITOR EVERY TIME I LOOK AT IT). IT'S MY FAULT THAT GENE LEFT OUT THE BOW AND ARROW, FOR WE WORKED WITH VERY SKETCHY INFORMATION I SUPPLIED PRIOR TO INTERVIEWING FREDERICK IN DEPTH.

GRAY BARKER'S NEWSLETTER is an official publication of the Saucers and Unexplained Celestial Events Research Society (SAUCERS). Published irregularly. 6 issues $6.00. By foreign air mail $12.00. Exchanges with other zines. Published by Saucerian Press, Inc., Box 2228, Clarksburg, WV 26301 US. Clippings and other saucerinformation needed.

Back issues available $1 ea: No. 3, Walton Abduction, Bender and MIB; No. 4, Ohio family sees Occupant, weird animal, Letter to Hynek and From Menzel, Reviews "8th Tower" & "Invisible College".

GRAY BARKER'S NEWSLETTER has no connection with NON-SCHEDULED NEWSLETTER, Vol. 23, No. 16.

Kollector's Korner & Personalities left out thish will return nextish.

Presstime comment: I predict that John Keel soon will announce receipt of a substantial grant from a leading foundation which will stress study of the Phenomena's impact on social and industrial programs rather than trying to catch a saucer. A spinoff from Keel's work in HEW.

yellow and it had pointed ears. Its body reminded him of the stalk of some huge ungainly plant, though it had remarkable physical power, coupled with the hypnotic effect the sing-song message imparted. He cried out in pain from the incisions and fright. Suddenly the eyes changed from yellow to red and seemed to rotate, and spinning orange circles emerged from them. His pain immediately ceased as the eyes created what obviously was an hypnotic effect, and he froze in his tracks, though his terror had also vanished. Frederick isn't sure, but he believes the "transfusion" lasted only about a minute, after which the creature suddenly released him, turned and ran up the hill in great leaping jumps, covering 25 ft. or more in each leap, like a modern "Spring-heeled Jack". He estimated the height of the leaps by noting it cleared a five-foot fence with about three feet to spare. At the hilltop it vanished into the woods.

The pain in his arm returned as he stared in the direction of the creature's spectacular exit. Then he heard a humming and whistling sound coming from the woods, as if the saucer the creature may have arrived in was taking off. He stumbled to his home, washed the wounded arm and put a bandage on it. Though the wound convinced him that he was sane and had actually experienced the horror, he doubted that anybody else would believe him. So he told his family he had been scratched by a briar and didn't see a doctor for fear of disclosure.

I sensed I was one of the few persons he had ever told of the happening, and that he trusted that I would not laugh at him. And suddenly I also realized a peculiar thing: the witness, while being questioned, was also interviewing me. I discovered that he was also obviously worried about some things he had read in books and articles by John Keel, and for the first time I was "getting to" the controlled terror that boiled just beneath his seemingly calm exterior. He asked me what I thought about a "pattern" Keel attributed to contactee and other UFO experiences. I reiterated what he must already have known about this subject: how these witnesses indeed often continued to have additional experiences, and how they often experienced personal difficulties -- though I played this down as much as possible, not wishing to contribute to his obvious worry.

At this point he told me of an even earlier sighting in which he believed he experienced a time distortion and related some recent sightings. Although some readers may scoff at his dramatic accounts, there is the independent sighting by his mother which indicates there was independent confirmation of UFO activity in the area. If you, the reader, are saying, "Well come on, you might as well end all this with the Men-In-Black bit," well, here we go:

Near the end of his Air Force enlistment Fredereck was assigned to temporary duty with NASA and given a security clearance. It is interesting to note (in connection with the MIB account) that while working for NASA he obviously encountered evidence of some secret project that dealt with UFOs. Although I did not press for information about this, he hinted there had been a lapse of security at NASA and that "several people were sacked" as a result. I got the impression he had seen plans or models of some sort of secret aircraft because he questioned me at length about what I knew of the history of the Avro Saucer, an early jet-powered airfoil taken over from the Canadian government by the U.S. and highly-touted in publicity releases by the Air Force. It seemed obvious at that time that the A.F. was aiming the publicity at those who believed in "flying saucers" of interplanetary origin to subtly persuade them that UFOs had an earthly and military origin (the AF "saucer" never flew successfully and is now on display at Wright Patterson Air Force Base).

About four months after his honorable discharge Frederick had the run-in with the MIB:

"I was living with my parents and slept on a cot near a window. One night sometime between 1:00 and 4:00 A.M. I was awakened by a red flash.

I thought the gas furnace had caught fire, so I raised up in bed and looked into the living room where my younger brother, Bill, was sleeping, and saw a small cannister about the size of an apple come bouncing across the living room floor. It was giving off a red colored vapor.

"I instinctively reached for my .38 pistol, which I always kept loaded under my pillow when living in the country, but a hand stopped me and I felt the prick of a needle in my left arm. I saw three men dressed in black turtle neck sweaters, slacks and what I thought were ski masks, entering the room through the window (I assume there was a fourth, the one that gave me the needle). One of them said, 'The dogs have been darted and everybody gased!' Another asked, 'What about this one? Will he remember?' The other replied, 'He's going out soon, he's half asleep! Don't worry about the needle! It will make his arm sore for a day or two, that's all!'

"Just as the red gas from the cannister was beginning to reach me, the men put on gas masks over the ones they had on, and the last thing I remember seeing was one man opening a suitcase with a tape recorder in it and another grabbing the cannister and stuffing it in his jacket pocket. Then they stuck something over my face and began to ask me questions, mainly about my UFO sightings and what I thought the UFOs actually were. I'm sure I was losing consciousness, for their other questions sounded very stupid, such as what did I know about time, and questions about the future."

Next morning nobody else in the household reported anything strange about the previous night, and Frederick assumed that the red vapor from the cannister had "put them out."

As I drove back to Clarksburg and home, the snow had stopped, and the late afternoon sunlight illuminated thousands of Christmas trees on the hillsides. The road was beginning to clear, and, back on the main highway I saw a crowd of parents and children gathering at the Terrace shopping center to see "Snow White and the Seven Dwarfs."

I mused about Mrs. Frederick's weird little demon man, stuffing weeds and dirt into his poke; Vegetable Man and the obvious similarity to the modern abductee, who is always the unwilling donor to some saucerian or galactic blood bank.

Frederick's MIB sounded to me very much like terrestrial visitors, with their talk of "gassing" and "darting the dogs." And there had been some incident involving his seeing something he shouldn't while with NASA.

I knew I would have to talk with Frederick again and try to penetrate further into the sub-stratum of what I still sensed was a massive, though unarticulated FEAR. Or maybe Frederick was one of THEM, either terrestrial, extraterrestrial or OTHERWISE, who had interviewed ME, as much as, or more so, than I had questioned him! More logically, however, Frederick was a man possessed, not by insanity, not by Christian devils, but by the Pattern. And he must exorcise this Fiend with a fighting spirit any mountain man carries in his brave heart. Frederick had himself become a UFO investigator. Perhaps he could prove they didn't exist. Perhaps he could prove that Keel's pattern didn't always come true. Perhaps all marriages didn't break up; perhaps not all percepients did not enter a mad world of unreality where hoarse voices croaked, "We are one!"

Then I forgot all this as I remembered the little girl, laughing and playing with our papers. The next time I visited Frederick, perhaps I could take her a nice picture book.

West Va. terminology: POKE: A paper bag. "My daddy went to the store and brought back a poke of candy."

NEWSLETTER readers may write to Jennings H. Frederick, Route #1, Box 126, Rivesville, WV 26588. Suggest courtesies such as stamped return envelopes and payment for any Xerox copies of files supplied. We always give addresses of witnesses when permission is granted. His phone is unlisted.

Letters to the Editor

Dear Gray:

The Fred Crisman summoned to testify in the Clay Shaw trial was the same Fred Crisman who was involved in the Tacoma Maury Island Affair, and the same Crisman who claimed to have shot his way out of a cave in Burma, receiving a hole the size of a dime in his arm from a "ray gun" wielded, (he said) by the dero. His exact words to me: "For God's sake, drop the Shaver cave stories! You don't know what you are dealing with here! He is the same Fred Crisman who offered to go into a cave in Texas and bring out some of the ancient machinery if I would send him $500 expense money.

It was not Clay Shaw who was ruined financially, personally and physically, it was Jim Garrison who was ruined. He was (as I told him in a letter) subjected to IRS audit, finally won the case in court but at tremendous financial cost -- which was the IRS goal in the first place. He was also libeled, framed in a drug ring, and hounded from office, finally losing out in a re-election run.

I have Garrison's letter stating that they were one and the same man. I also have my answer to Garrison, predicting that Crisman could not be subpeoned, that he was CIA, and tremendously powerful.

There is a definite link between flying saucers, the Shaver Mystery, The Kennedy(s) assasinations, Watergate and Fred Crisman. There is one common denominator for everything that is happening in the world today. That common denominator is right where Shaver said it was -- no matter whether you prefer caverns or the lower astral or another dimension.

Rap

(Ray Palmer, Rt. 2, Box 36, Amherst, Wisconsin 54406)

Dear Gray;

My usual fee for allowing my handsome countenance to be used on the cover of scurilous publications is $5,000. However, in this case you will be an exception. I have instructed my lawyer to sue you for everything you've got.

Despite my valiant efforts to reduce everything to the simplest possible language my "message" seems to float majestically over the heads of all my readers...except Vallee. He borrows freely from me and now even Dr. Hynek has taken up the habit (see Edge of Reality), tho they may actually be unaware of how deeply my gilded words have infiltrated their consciousnesses. Line after line in Vallee's The Invisible College (TIC) are only slightly paraphrased from OTH and Our Haunted Planet. The latter books dealt extensively with Fatima, Lourdes, the Mormons, etc. at a time when Vallee (in Passport to Magonia) showed a strange reluctance to examine the religious implications of the phenomenon. The ideas he now extolls, though in a vague, diaphanous way, were fully explored by me in the 1960's and graphically discussed in the books I published five or six years ago. During that period, you may recall, Vallee, Hynek and others in their crowd were attacking me openly and pooh-poohing the "occult connection." Now that they are executing a classic right angle turn, they are adopting my once-hated concepts and claiming them as their own. Vallee has even lifted some of my favorite citations (Oahspe, The Book of the Mormon, etc.) although he obviously has not read the books I cite.

Dr. Hynek first revealed the existence of The Invisible College in 1966. He has had ten years to get his act together. I expected Vallee's book to reveal the results of ten years of effort. Instead TIC could have been written by any NY hack with my books at his elbow. No vast international network of scientists was necessary, nor are they even dimly apparent in TIC. Only one episode suggests their presence...the scientists in Europe and France who were taken in by the obviously terrestrial UMMO affair (See my article in Saga, June, 1973). The book is part Vallee, part Keel and part bullshit. But the Invisible College is just as invisible as ever. It apparently exists in the same way that Project Blue Book existed. More a myth than a fact. A handful of scientists are named but their contributions are uncertain. Vallee seems to rely more on Aime Michel, who is a brilliant fellow but no scientist (he's the Brad Steiger of France). One of his favorite cronies, Jacques Bergier, recently did a rewrite of Our Haunted Planet and called it Secret Doors of the Earth.

From TIC and Edge of Reality I gather that Hynek and Vallee are now at roughly the same point that I reached in 1968-1969, but they are proceeding slowly, possibly because they instinctively realize -- and fear -- that if they pursue the evidence to its logical conclusion they will have killed off their beloved boondoggle. The simple truth is: there is nothing whatsoever to the UFO phenomenon; there is nothing to be gained by a scientific study of the matter; the ETH is nothing but a trick...a propaganda device...that has been foisted upon us. Historically, the overall phenomena has done considerable damage to the human race and is responsible for the deaths of many millions of people. It is human to indulge in wishful thinking and hope that it is leading us somewhere, but it has always led us down dead ends to destruction and I don't think the situation is suddenly going to change. Vallee has absolutely no sense of history and Hynek is, of course, completely out of his element in this kind of study. Hynek has spent ten years trying to raise millions of dollars for a scientific study of UFOs. In articles published in 1967-68, I pointed out that the U.S. had already spent millions on the subject and that no amount of money and no number of scientists could ever solve "the mystery". Now, at least, Vallee has swung to that point of view. He has finally recognized the fundamentals ...that a subjective phenomenon cannot be explored with technology.

On the other hand, if the ETists are right...if UFOs are real machines from some other planet then the historical record suggests only one proper avenue of approach. The subject is a matter exclusively for a highly trained highly secret group of Intelligence agencies, and not a matter for amateur investigators. If UFOs are real, then the situation is so grave that all amateur groups should be ruthlessly crushed, all UFO news should be censored, and the general population should be kept in total ignorance as long as possible. Apparently the government did try to implement such a program on a modest scale in the early 1950's but it was fragmented, poorly financed and inefficient. The phenomenon itself has so many built-in contradictions it doesn't need any outside help. If the government had found real cause for alarm, you can be sure that people like Keyhoe, Coral Lorenzen, Jim Moseley, etc., would have been jailed on trumped-up charges and no civilian UFO movement would never have had a chance to organize.

Here's a chart I drew up in an effort to cleanly define "Middle Ufology" and all that. You may use it as you see fit (The paper is too harsh to use in the bathroom).

My famous beard is gone again. The C.I.A. put some powder in my shoes which caused all my hair to fall out. Duplantier's drawing is really unnecessarily flattering. What did he use for a model? That old Post Office poster of me? Best.....john a. keel

(john a. keel, Box 351, Murray Hill Station, NY, NY 10016)

Dear John: I'm glad you're suing for everything I've got instead of 5Gs. Since my net worth is about (-37¢) you will owe ME money, but I'll settle for a beer. Duplantier drew your likeness from old SAUCER NEWS issues. Now that your appearance has vastly changed, I suspect you are the anonymous person who has been reporting to me word-for-word what has transpired in recent secret NICAP meetings. Your chart, which differs somewhat from the Greenfieldian version, is reproduced on the following page. Your humble servant, Gray

SPECIALIZED RESEARCH, INC.

Box 351
P. O. Murray Hill Station
New York, N. Y 10016

RADICAL LEFT	CONSERVATIVE LEFT	MIDDLE UFOLOGY	CONSERVATIVE RIGHT	RADICAL RIGHT
Creighton Vallee Keel Clark	U.S. Government Bergier Menzels Klass	Hynek Flying Saucer Review	APRO Blum SAGA UFO Reports	Contactee Cults NICAP MUFON Friedman, Stanford, Keyhoe, etc.
Premise: The ETH is untenable. All UFO manifestations can be explained in philosophical and psychological terms as part of an environmental mechanism for producing beliefs and myths.	Premise: The ETH is untenable. All UFO manifestations can be explained by mundane phenomena.	Premise: All possible explanations should be equally considered.	Premise: The ETH is the most likely explanation.	Premise: The ETH is the only acceptable explanation.

The Extraterrestrial Hypothesis (ETH) has always been the core of the UFO belief and is therefore the best criterion for assessing the various factions of the so-called Ufological Movement. NICAP, for example, has always claimed to be "conservative" because it excluded all other explanations. Actually its basic position is the same as the contactee cults. Those who have dismissed the ETH in favor of more complex concepts belong at the opposite pole or the Radical Left. Eccentric theories, such as those of Palmer, Shaver, various religious groups etc. cannot be fitted onto this scale.

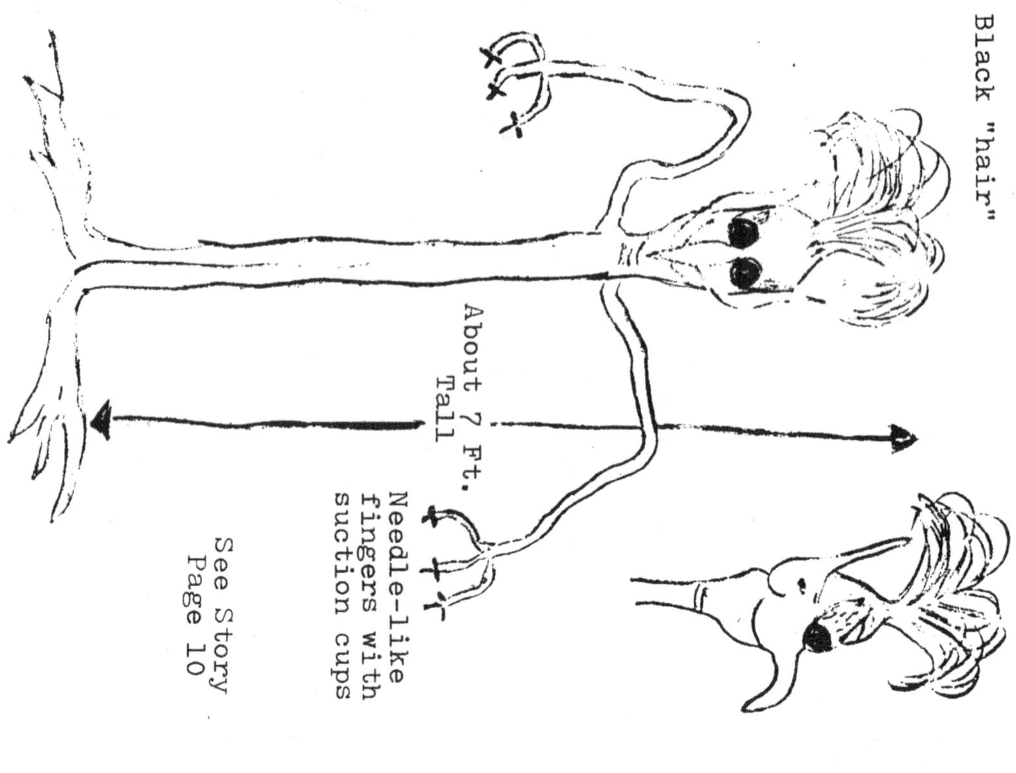

Black "hair"

About 7 Ft. Tall

Needle-like fingers with suction cups

See Story Page 10

Semi-abductee Jennings H. Frederick's drawing of green creature encountered in West Virginia, with side view of head above right.

A pattern of weird UFO events has plagued the witness since the late 1960's.

Don't laugh! For Vegetable Man could get YOU if you don't watch out!

From
Saucerian Press, Inc.
Box 2228
Clarksburg, WV 26301
U.S. Planet Earth

THIRD CLASS MAIL

Postperson, please deliver to:

"The dogs have been darted and everybody gased!"
---- The MIB

(See story Page 10)

www.ingramcontent.com/pod-product-compliance
Lightning Source LLC
Chambersburg PA
CBHW081135300726
48982CB00005B/975

9781955087315